EVE BUNTING

The In-Between Days

illustrated by Alexander Pertzoff

HarperCollins*Publishers*

The In-Between Days

Text copyright © 1994 by Edward D. Bunting and Anne E. Bunting, Trustees of the
Edward D. Bunting and Anne E. Bunting Family Trust
Illustrations copyright © 1994 by Alexander Pertzoff
Library of Congress Cataloging-in-Publication Data
Bunting, Eve, date
    The in-between days / Eve Bunting ; illustrated by Alexander Pertzoff.
       p.   cm.
    Summary: Reluctant to see any changes in his life on Dove Island, eleven-year-old
George tries to get rid of his father's new girlfriend.
    ISBN 0-06-023609-4. — ISBN 0-06-023612-4 (lib. bdg.)
    [1. Single parent family—Fiction. 2. Islands—Fiction.]   I. Pertzoff, Alexander, ill.
II. Title.
PZ7.B91527Ip   1994   93-45674
[Fic]—dc20   CIP
                                                                              AC

Typography by Al Cetta
· 5   6   7   8   9   10
❖

To my friends,
the librarians and teachers of Michigan
—E. B.

To Merry Nasser,
with love and gratitude
—A. P.

The
In-Between
Days

Chapter 1

It was sometime in August when Caroline first came to the island. My little brother, James, and I noticed her getting off the ferryboat with the rest of the tourists. When we saw her cross the street to Dad's bike rental shop we tagged behind.

"How much to rent a bike for the day?" she asked Dad.

"Fifteen dollars," he said, and she said, "Okay."

She chose a blue ten-speed and took her ID and driver's license out of a red backpack to show to Dad.

"Caroline Best, 12 Shore Road, St. Ann's," he read aloud.

"Right," she said.

While he wrote it down, she turned to us. "I hear there are good fudge shops on this island."

"A jillion of them," James said.

"But I bet you boys know the best one, right?"

"Right," I said. "Annie's is prime."

"We can show you if you like," James offered, and I knew he was hoping for a free chunk of fudge. James is a greedy little turkey.

"Great," Caroline said.

We got our bikes and rode with her along Main Street. Because it was summer, the island bulged with tourists. The horse trams were busy and the souvenir and shell shops swarmed with people. The air was sweet with the warm smells of fresh fudge and horse droppings. Although the pooper scooper guys in their white uniforms were hard at work behind the horses, it wasn't easy for them to keep up. Those horses have some output.

The three of us pulled in at Annie's and James and I watched the bikes while Caroline went inside. She bought double chocolate pecan delight and we leaned on our bikes and munched.

"Do you boys live on the island all-year round?" Caroline asked.

"Yup," I said.

"Isn't it lonely in winter when the tourists leave?"

"Nope." James's cheeks bulged. "We like it best when the tourists go."

That kid is *rude*. I give him a look. *She's* a tourist, dumbo. To Caroline I said, "He's only five. His name is James." I touched my chest. "I'm George. I'm eleven."

Caroline smiled. "I'm Caroline, and I'm thirty-two." She had great gappy teeth, the kind you see on the happy pumpkin face, except prettier. Her hair was long and brown as a horse's mane. I decided she wasn't as cute as Debbie O'Jibway, who is the all-time cutest girl in fifth grade. But for someone old Caroline looked really good.

"How many people live on the island year-round?" she asked me.

"Forty-three families including ours," I said.

James licked his fingers one by one. "If you like we could show you the best ice-cream shop on the island too," he said. "It's down the street."

Caroline laughed. "That sounds like an idea."

We showed her the sights of Dove Island as we biked

along. Bleeker's Fort up on the hill, where they shoot off the cannons each Fourth of July; the Bay View Hotel, where once they made a movie and put up humongous tents on the front lawn.

James and Caroline and I sat on the bay wall to eat our ice-cream cones. The tops of the masts of the old sailing ship that sank there in 1832 poked out of the water.

"Her name's *Miss Julia*, and she was a schooner," James told Caroline. "Our mom's name was Julia, too. She died just after I was born." James was speaking in the sad little voice he always has when he speaks about Mom. "Georgie was six."

"I'm sorry," Caroline said, and I could tell she really was. I decided right away that she was nice.

I helped James mop the ice-cream drips off his T-shirt, then showed Caroline the road that goes around the island. "It's only four miles. If you stay on it you can't get lost," I said.

She waved and we watched her go.

The ferry wasn't in yet when she brought the bike back to the shop.

"The island's so beautiful," she told Dad, "and when

you get past Main Street you hardly see anyone. No Cars Allowed. That's what makes the difference. I used to live in Chicago and I can't believe this quiet."

Dad grinned. "It's not exactly Chicago, that's for sure. What made you leave?"

"My husband and I got divorced," Caroline said. "I needed to get away. But now I think I need to get back. I miss the big city."

"St. Ann's *is* a big city," I said.

Caroline smiled. "Not hardly."

James pointed out of the bike shop window. "Here comes the Island Rover."

We heard the ferry whistle, and when we looked we could see it nudging the dock with its square white nose. The dock swayed and water rolled over the wooden planks. The crowds of tourists swayed, too, screaming and laughing the way they do every day.

"Come back and see us," Dad told Caroline.

"There's another road cuts right across the island," I added quickly. "It's neat, like a jungle. You'd like it."

"Oh, I think I need to see that." Caroline picked up her backpack. "Thanks."

We watched her go across and stand with the rest of

the tourists who were heading back to St. Ann's.

I liked her a lot that first day and the next time she came back, too. I thought she and Dad were just having nice, friendly conversations in the bike shop.

My friend Tyler Flaherty says I was naive, which is just another word for dumb. Anyway, I never suspected that Dad and Caroline were getting serious about each other.

When I did, I stopped liking Caroline real fast.

Chapter 2

I knew they were getting serious about each other the day we went to the point for a picnic.

Caroline had come to the island four Saturdays in a row by then. The week before last Dad closed up the shop and came biking with us.

"You should have been suspicious right then, ninny," Tyler told me. "Your Dad shutting up the shop? And on a Saturday?"

Tyler was right. I'd been a ninny, naive, dumb . . . all of those things.

But last Saturday when we went on the picnic I got suspicious for real.

Dad had brought his binoculars and was watching the sandpipers pecking their way along the water's edge. After a few minutes he put the binoculars down and turned to Caroline, who was sitting next to him on the grass.

"Do you know your eyes are the same brown as a sandpiper's feathers?" he said softly. "Your eyes have little golden flecks and streaks in them too."

Caroline made a face and laughed. "Oh, David. Honestly. Bird feathers!"

"Bird legs," James shouted. "Caroline has bird legs and a yellow beak." He says her name as if it's three names, Car-o-line.

"Peep, peep," Caroline piped, and then Dad said, "Caroline is beautiful."

Just like that. Imagine? I was eating a plum and I almost choked. I looked up and Caroline and Dad were staring at each other and Caroline wasn't laughing anymore. I knew something was happening. I knew then, all right.

That night I was relieved when we put her on the ferry. Good riddance, I thought. We're safe again.

But of course she came back.

And back.

Now she's coming every weekend.

Today, when we got up we saw that it had snowed in the night. James and I wandered down to the dock to see Mr. Consorto and his helpers load the tram horses onto the ten o'clock ferry. They have fields and stables for them in St. Ann's. Mr. Flaherty, Tyler's dad, jokes about how the horses are like the rich folks who summer on the island in the big, fancy houses. "The only difference is those gee-gees work for a living," he says.

Most of the other kids are here, watching too. The horses stumble up the ramp onto the Island Rover and when we wave them good-bye we know summer is really over.

The bay is awash with floating chunks of ice and the ferry makes only two crossings a day now, once in the morning, once in the evening.

"Is there ever so much ice that the ferry can't get through?" Caroline asks the next Saturday when she comes as usual.

"Sure," James tells her proudly. "When the bay's totally frozen it can't come. And two other times, just before the bay freezes up and just after it starts to melt. The ferry can't come then, either. The bay's dangerous. All bits of sharp ice and stuff. So we get to be marooned."

Ever since Dad read us *Treasure Island* James has loved the word "marooned" and he repeats it a couple of times just for the sound of it.

"You are really marooned?" Caroline asks Dad, and I see her shudder.

"Only for a little while," Dad says. "Don't worry."

My stomach jumps. Why would he think she'd worry? She wouldn't be here.

"But sometimes we get marooned for a long time," I say quickly. "Weeks. Months, even. Nobody can come here and we can't go there. There's nothing to do. Talk about lonely. It's totally lonely then."

We're sitting on the bay wall again. The ferry has carried only seven passengers this morning and Caroline was one of them. Already the island is getting its deserted island look.

"But then we make our ice bridge," James says cheerfully, "and we can cross to St. Ann's any time we like. It's fun."

Caroline frowns. "An ice bridge? What do you mean?"

"Across the bay." Dad squeezes her hand and smiles down at her. I hate it when he does that. "We call it a bridge, though it isn't really. Our ice tester goes across and shows us where the ice is thick enough so we can go from the island to the mainland. I guess it is a kind of bridge because if you step off it you're in the water . . ."

"Harry the Needle—" James interrupts, "We call him that because he has this big long silver needle that he sticks into the ice to see if it's thick enough to walk on." James stops for breath, then starts again. I swear, James is like a windup toy. He runs down, but then some crazy invisible person goes behind him and cranks him up again. "Even horses can cross. Even snowmobiles, and before that, when we're marooned, we call that time the 'in-between days.' We're in between . . ." He stops. Not exactly sure. Then spreads his arms. "We're in between everything."

"In between time and space, bay and sky," Dad says. "You'll see." He jumps from the wall and pulls Caroline down beside him, holding her for a second. I hate it even more when he does that.

"We put markers down so we know exactly where the bridge is," Dad adds. His lips touch her hair.

"In fact, maybe you'll even help us with that this year, Caro."

I pitch a rock into the bay and watch the ripples curl and swirl, the way fudge curls when it's turning soft on the machines in the fudge shop windows. I wish we were marooned now. Us on this side and Caroline on the other. But we aren't. The island's still open. Worse, worst of all, next Saturday Caroline's coming to our house for the first time. Dad has asked her. She'll be on the early ferry. I smell danger.

Dad and James and I are in the kitchen and Dad keeps looking at the clock. Now he jumps up and says, "Time to go, boys. The Rover will be here any minute."

He takes his coat from the rack by the door, tosses James's jacket to him and mine to me. I keep working on the model airplane I'm putting together on the kitchen table and let my jacket fall on the braided rug. Model airplanes are my full-time specialty.

James has struggled into his jacket already, and he plops down on the floor to pull on his boots. "Aren't you coming, Georgie? Aren't you coming to meet Caroline?"

"Yeah," I say, and dawdle over setting the plane on the spread newspaper, capping the glue.

Dad and James are antsy with excitement as I lace up my boots.

There's been a new snowfall in the night, and we trudge in single file along the deserted street.

By now most of the shops are closed for the season, except for the True Value market, which is open all year. The shutters on the shell emporium are safely fastened. Every single fudge shop is boarded up, including Annie's. Snow is piled thick on windowsills and the island is smothered in silence. Dad's bike shop is closed too. The snow has been cleared from in front of it, because he and I are down here a lot fixing up the rentals so they'll be ready for summer. Actually, we're not down here so much now, not since Caroline.

We're passing the big wooden block of the ferry building and the spread of the icy bay opens up to us, the houses and church spires of St. Ann's on the other side.

"There she is," Dad says.

The Island Rover's nosing its way through the floating ice, butting against the dock. Its horn blasts. "I see Car-o-line," James yells, and starts waving like a lunatic.

Dad, the dork, is jumping and waving, too.

I stick my hands in my jacket pocket. "It's not too hard to see her," I say grouchily. "She's the only one on the boat."

"Do you think she'll like our house, Dad? Do you?" James asks. "I think she will, don't you, Dad?"

James's nose is running and his hair spikes out from under his knitted cap. Seeing him look like such an idiot should turn Caroline off, but I bet it won't. "Who cares if she doesn't like the house? It's ours. She doesn't have to live in it, does she?" I ask.

Dad looks down at me. "Be nice to her, Georgie," he says, and I shrug.

I have been nice. If you ask me, I've been too nice.

Chapter 3

We walk home, and now our parade has an extra person in it, with Caroline behind Dad, and James almost clipping her heels, he's so anxious to catch her up on what's been happening since he saw her last. He never shuts up.

She's brought this big canvas bag that Dad's carrying. The bag has me worried. She's just coming for the day, isn't she? That's what he told us. So what's with the luggage?

When we get home Caroline doesn't look down her nose at anything, or gush over it, which would have been worse. All she does is nod. "It is nice, James."

I look around the kitchen too, imagining I'm Caroline seeing it for the first time. Our old black stove that swallows firewood is clear of its usual mess of pots and pans. It gives off so much heat we have to sit away from it, even on the coldest nights. "Change that stove for one of the new ones?" Mom had asked. "It's in better shape than I am."

I blink, remembering. Mom was right. The stove's here and she's lying dead in the island churchyard.

Our corduroy couch is saggy in the middle, and I see that Dad has smartened it up for the occasion with the green afghan Mom crocheted. I think I remember her crocheting it, but maybe not. The kitchen clock with its heavy brass pendulum is thumping away. Dad always tells James not to watch that pendulum because it will hypnotize him out of his head.

I sit down at the table with its four chairs and the green glass jar filled with dried flowers in the center. Everything's tidied and dusted for Caroline's coming—even the flowers. A spider's been webbing up in there for ages and ages. He's gone now.

The only thing to spoil it is the mess of newspapers and glue I've left on the table. Too bad.

Caroline has unzipped her jacket and Dad hangs it on the hook. She holds her hands out to the stove. I see she's wearing a brown skirt and a blouse with red and yellow stripes, and boots that go up to her knees. Her hair is held back with some kind of elastic flowered thing.

"I hope you guys like roast chicken," she says, "and sweet potato casserole and chocolate cake with double fudge frosting, because that's what I brought." She nods toward the bag that Dad set on the chair.

"Roast chicken. Yum!" Dad closes his eyes as if he's about to faint or something and James claps his hands.

"Double fudge frosting. That's my very favorite."

Caroline beams. "Great."

"*Everything* is James's very favorite," I say, so she won't feel so smart about herself. "You know how he is with the fudge." I give James an elbow dig. "At the picnic you said hot dogs were your favorite things. He likes everything," I repeated.

"I don't know if I can fit 'everything' in my bag next time I come, James," Caroline says, "but I'll give it a try."

Those words, 'next time,' don't cheer me up much.

Of course Dad sees Caroline in St. Ann's. I don't know how often.

Caroline works at Fellowes Hardware. Since Dad is a part-time over-the-winter painter, he goes to Fellowes a lot. He gets a lot of jobs sprucing up the insides of the bed-and-breakfasts and the Bay View Hotel. They're closed till next summer, but the owners leave Dad the keys. A lot of the island people don't have off-season jobs, but Dad has this and the bike shop too.

He goes to St. Ann's for the stuff he needs—rollers, tire patches, whatever. Before Caroline he used to buy everything in Carpenters' Hardware in St. Ann's, but he's changed.

On one of the Saturday afternoons he and Caroline and James and I are sitting around the table in the kitchen. We're putting together the jigsaw puzzle Caroline brought for James. Some kind of music is playing on the radio. The old-fashioned kind from a ballroom or something.

"Did you know Mom and Dad met at a church dance in St. Ann's," I say, though nobody has asked me. "Mom was wearing a fuzzy pink sweater and she had a big bow in her hair."

James chimes up, "And it came loose . . ."

I interrupt. "And when the caller called, 'Change partners, do-si-do,' you wouldn't, right, Dad? You wouldn't change partners."

Caroline smiles. "Your dad told me. It was very romantic."

"It was sad when she died," James says, and Caroline touches his cheek. "I know."

She reaches her hand over the model of Tyrannosaurus rex that James had set on the table. Her fingers curl warm around mine, then let go.

I tell Tyler about it on Monday morning when we're on the ferry going across to school.

"I really didn't want to take her hand, but it would have been rude not to."

All the Dove Island kids go to school on the early ferry and come back on the last one, so I keep my voice low in case any of the others can hear.

"And my dad's so goopy around her, I can hardly stand it," I add.

Tyler shrugs. "So? We're both goopy over Debbie O'Jibway, aren't we? And kind of goopy over Marguerite Boniface."

The ferry veers a little to miss a hump of floating ice, big as a tabletop. The ice dances away across the black water.

I yell at James to come stand next to me. That kid's always wandering off. He pretends not to hear.

"We don't hold hands with Debbie, though. We don't tell her all the time how glad we are to see her," I say.

Tyler looks gloomy. "Only because she won't let us."

Caroline and Dad hold hands a lot. It's almost as if they're glued together.

"I don't think she's that bad-looking," John Peterson says. He's been listening, even though I was almost whispering.

I sniff. "Who asked you?"

The island kids know what's going on. They see Dad meeting her at the ferry and kissing her good-bye.

"Hi Caroline, hi Mr. Bowser," they say. Mr. Bowser is Dad. They give him and Caroline and us sly little smiles.

When Caroline's not here, Dad talks to us about how much he loves us and how nothing will ever change that.

He talks about Mom.

One night when we're playing Monopoly he says, "Your Mom loved Monopoly. She used to buy up all the hotels. She was a big business kind of kid at heart." He smiles in a remembering way.

"It was awful when she died. In a way, all the days since have been in-between days."

James screws up his face. "What do you mean? You mean marooned?"

Dad grins. "Not exactly, but it's as if we're waiting, you know, waiting for real life to begin again."

"I don't get it," James says.

But I do.

I know Dad loves us. I know he loved Mom. But still, he's found someone to put in her place. He thinks the in-between days might end.

Caroline's here every single Saturday except one when she had to go to the dentist. It's hard to believe Saturday used to be my favorite day of the week.

I stay away from them as much as I can. When she's here I sit in my room and work on my airplanes. I've got thirty-three classic and modern designs. I've got Future of Flight and the Voyager, and I'm painting them with acrylic flash paints, turning them into real fine state-of-the-art jobs.

On one of those Saturday afternoons I come down to the kitchen, soundless in my socks, and see Caroline and Dad sitting side by side on the couch, on Mom's afghan. They're kissing.

I stop two steps up. My heart is thumping.

"Promise me you won't get into it with him," Caroline says when they come up for oxygen. I know they're going on with some conversation that had stopped when the kiss started. I know, too, that they're talking about me.

I move back a step and press against the wall.

"There have only been the three of you for so long," Caroline says, "and he resents me. It's natural. Give him time."

"I'm worried about that, though," Dad says.

I peek forward and see Caroline pick up the blue-and-white striped scarf she's knitting for James. It's a terrible-looking scarf, all holes and dropped stitches. Some parts of it are skinny, some are fat. I don't think she's a very good knitter. My mom was a crocheter. Everyone says the afghan is a masterpiece.

"James was so little when his mom died. He doesn't

remember," Caroline says. "George does. No wonder it's hard for him."

I go silently back to my room and lean my forehead against the wallpaper that Mom and Dad had put up years and years ago. It has toy soldiers on it, the kind with britches and muskets. Round and round they stomp. Through my tears they blur together into raggedy columns.

What makes Caroline think she knows anything about me?

That night we walk with her to the ferry the way we always do. Then we trudge home, the three of us, and it's so cold that the stars seem to snap. A ghost moon sits pale above the dark-and-white patchwork of the bay. The ice looks so still, but I know everything is moving out there, the pieces fitting themselves together.

Long icicles hang from the roofs along Main Street, shining and silver as daggers. I remember how Mom used to break one off for me to dip in cranberry juice. I'd wait for it to turn pink. It never did, but it sure tasted good. Caroline was right. I remember a lot of things.

I snap an icicle from the windowsill of our bike shop for James, and carry it carefully, though I don't think we have any juice. Snow has built up around the bike shop door. I miss being there. I miss the smells, the warmth from the little fire. I miss being with Dad. The three of us were okay before she came.

Cold burns my chest and hurts above my eyes.

James starts to whimper the way he does when he gets tired, and Dad hoists him up.

I'm walking behind their shadowy shapes and I'm thinking, Why do things have to change? If only Caroline would go away and never come back.

Chapter 4

It's December now, a Friday night. Dad, James, and I are in our pajamas, sitting around the table drinking hot cocoa before we go to bed.

The kitchen is so toasty warm we don't even need robes. The stove glows, the clock thumps, the outside world is white and quiet.

"Would it be okay with you guys if I invited Caroline for Christmas?" Dad asks. He's turning his mug in his hands. When he looks up I see he has a brown cocoa mustache just like James's.

"Sure," James says enthusiastically. "That would be

prime perfect." James has picked up "prime" from me and added his own second part, even though I told him he didn't need it. "Prime IS perfect," I said.

"Prime perfect is even better," he told me back.

Dad's looking at me now. "Georgie, I know Christmas has always been special for us, but Caroline's family is in Chicago. It's hard getting there this time of year. It would be sad for her to be alone."

"Bring her here." James slurps up the last of his cocoa. "I bet Caroline gives prime perfect presents. I bet she . . . "

"Will we still go to Christmas service and take Mom her candles?" I ask, my voice so low that James blurts, "What, Georgie? What did you say?"

But Dad hears.

"She'll want to come," I add. "Caroline."

"To the service, yes, but not to Mom's grave, unless we ask her," Dad says.

James is listening now. "I think Caroline *should* come to Mom's grave. Mom would have liked Caroline. They'd have been friends."

"How come you're so sure?" I ask. "You didn't even know Mom."

"I did too. I did and I know she was nice." James is ready to cry, and already I'm mad at myself.

"Sorry," I mutter. "Of course you knew her. She held you all the time."

"About Caroline and Christmas," Dad asks quietly. "Is it okay?"

"I guess," I say.

I think Dad asks her the next day, and I figure she says yes, since she thanks James and me for including her. She's brought an Advent calendar and she explains to us the way it works. There's a picture of a house that looks like ours, all covered with snow, except it's bigger and it's got lots of numbered windows with shutters on them, and a golden front door.

"You follow the numbers and you open one shutter every day from now till Christmas. You open the door last."

Since it's already December fifth, there are five shutters that need to be opened right off.

James opens the first one, and there's a cardboard sheep behind it. You can lift the sheep out and there's a prop in back so it can stand up.

"Put it on the mantel," Caroline tells him. "By the

time Christmas comes we'll have a whole nativity scene. Go ahead, George, you open the second one."

I shake my head. "Let James," I say. It really bugs me the way she says, " . . . we'll have . . . ." We, as if she's part of our family.

James gets another sheep and two lambs and a dog. He likes the dog a lot. He calls it Beauty.

"Your turn tomorrow," he tells me, but already I know I want nothing to do with this moving toward Christmas. Some part of me knows that Christmas is scary this year. There's a feeling in the air—an excitement. Is Dad going to sit with James and me one night around the kitchen table and say, "Would it be okay with you guys if Caroline and I got engaged?"

Marilee O'Jibway and that guy from St. Ann's got engaged last Christmas. He gave her a diamond ring as big as a cherry, and Mrs. Boniface said it was fake, because no guy who worked in a bank could afford that kind of real diamond, not unless he robbed the bank.

"Do people often get engaged at Christmas?" I ask Tyler casually at recess the next Monday. "I mean, is it a big tradition or something?"

Tyler looks blank. "I don't know. I've never been engaged."

But something is going on. I wish James would stop opening those shutters on the calendar, because every time he opens one Christmas gets closer.

The next Saturday as the ferry comes in, James rushes to hug Caroline and tell her what new figures are on the mantel.

There are only thirteen more days now till Christmas; four more days of school. Our class is making calendars for presents. We've put in the moons and the tides and all the holidays. The kindergartners are making jewel boxes out of popsicle sticks.

"Mine's for Caroline. Do you think she'll like it?" James asks.

"You've asked me that a million times," I tell him. "She'll like it. She'll be crazy about it."

James nods. "It IS pretty prime perfect, I have to say."

Caroline has finished knitting James's scarf. It's the worst-looking scarf in the world, all holes and ridges.

"Never mind," she says, cheerful as can be, winding it around James's neck and pushing him in front of her to our big wood-framed mirror. "A mistake shows something is handmade and that makes it special. A person has to love a person to go to all that bother, not to mention do all that crummy knitting."

She hugs James and James hugs her back.

"I like mistakes, Caroline," he says, and she laughs.

I haven't seen any signs of Caroline making a scarf for me.

Dad and James are busy fixing up the spare room for Caroline to use at Christmas. They're throwing out junk that has been stored there forever and ever. I help too, when Dad asks me, but I'm not very enthusiastic. We carry down an old desk and a marked-up chest of drawers.

I tell Tyler about how we're fixing up the spare room. He glances sideways at me. "If they get married and have a new baby they'll need that room anyway," he says.

Oh no, surely they wouldn't.

"Shut up," I tell him. We're standing on the ferry landing. The Island Rover is late because the ice is really piling up on the bay. We're muffled like arctic explorers and we stomp our feet to try to keep warm. John Peterson's holding the hand heater his grandma sent him from California. The thing's useless but he makes a big deal out of it. Debbie O'Jibway has new white fur earmuffs that are real cute against her black hair.

"Let's grab them off her head and play catch with them," Tyler suggests. But I'm not in the mood for games. In fact I'm thinking hard.

Today, walking to the ferry I'd seen something. There was a dead mouse stretched out on a snowbank. He was frozen stiff, his gray fur plastered to his bones so he was no thicker than my thumb.

I picked him up by his tail and twirled him around. His grin was a death grin. Inside my head something began whirling, too.

Wouldn't he make a great Christmas present for Caroline? But I couldn't give him to her. That would be too awful.

I put him back and covered him with a shallow sprinkle of snow. I marked the spot with a long, straight twig, though, just in case I changed my mind. It's a mouse grave marker.

Now standing waiting for the ferry, hearing Tyler say, "If they have a new baby . . . ," I'm feeling desperate. If this romance keeps going, who knows where it will end? I've got to get rid of her.

And I think about the mouse.

Chapter 5

Tonight when we're having a supper of hamburger and beans in the kitchen I notice the dried flowers have disappeared from the center of the kitchen table.

"What happened to them?" I ask.

"I put them up in Caroline's room to make it pretty," James says, all pleased with himself.

Dad ruffles James's hair. "That was a great idea, James."

"Those flowers are house property," I say. "Why didn't somebody ask me?"

Dad gives me a serious look. "What would you have said, George? Would you have said no?"

I grab my plate and take it across to the sink. "Nobody asked me anyway, so what's the difference?"

The Advent calendar shutters are almost all open now, and the nativity scene has most of its animals in place. There are even three angels. The main characters are still missing, the wise men, Mary and Joseph and the baby. We haven't had the stars or the gifts or the camels yet either. The shutters look a little bent. I'm sure James has been peeking behind them, although he shakes his head furiously when I accuse him.

"Deck the walls with balls of holly," he sings joyously as he and I do the dishes.

"Put the glasses away," I tell him.

Afterward Dad does what he does almost every night. He puts on his jacket and his boots and clumps out into the snow to call Caroline. We don't have a phone, but there's one down at the True Value store. He looks happy when he comes back. I swear he looks like some soppy twelfth-grader.

"Caroline sends her love," he tells James and me.

"And I send mine to her." James blows kisses into the air. He's such a dweeb.

———

I check on my mouse marker every day. It's getting shorter and shorter as the snow gets deeper.

Today is Thursday, December seventeenth, the last day of school, and just the tip of the marker is showing.

When the last bell for the last class rings I take the calendar I've made, the one with the moon and the tides and everything on it, and give it to Mrs. Yokum. She'd been my teacher last year and I like her a lot.

"Oh, George, it's lovely. But don't you want it for your Dad for Christmas?"

"It's okay. I bought him a book on shore birds," I say, which is true.

As soon as I get on the ferry, Tyler asks, "Where's your calendar?"

He's sitting on his because the slatted seat is wet with icy spray. His calendar isn't so great to begin with, so I don't think sitting on it is going to make much difference to the way it looks.

"I gave it to Mrs. Yokum," I say.

"How come?"

"Because."

The bay is heavy with swells that rock in under the slabs of ice and the Island Rover rocks with them. Tyler and I get up and stand by the railing watching Dove

Island come closer, a white hump in the black water. Now we can see the Bay View Hotel lying like a beached whale, dead on the rocks.

Debbie and Marguerite and the rest of the island girls are standing in a tight little knot beside the rack of life jackets. We know from past experience not to try to get in good with them. Once they graciously accepted a sugar doughnut from me that I bought at the concession stand, but Tyler and I agree that we can't be buying them stuff all the time. If a girl needs *that* to make her like us, then she's not worth it. Of course we know Debbie O'Jibway is really worth anything. The real reason we don't try to buy her favors is that a doughnut costs ninety-five cents. We can't afford that kind of money.

Tyler's younger sisters, Heather and Iona, are squeezed with James between us and the railings. They're talking about Christmas and presents and about tomorrow, when all the islanders go up to Dobb's Wood to cut down our Christmas trees.

"Caroline's coming to us for Christmas," James tell them, very importantly. And Iona says, "You're lucky. Our dad doesn't have a girlfriend."

Tyler bops their heads. "That's because we have a mom, you dumbos."

It's funny. James and I used to think the other kids were sorry for us. They had moms and we didn't. Now they're curious, and even envious. We're the ones with the excitement.

I have a grip on the back of James's scarf—Caroline's scarf—which I knotted tightly under his collar. He keeps trying to shake my hand off and he's yelling, "Don't!" and "Let go," over his shoulder, but I ignore him. He's holding the popsicle-stick jewel box wrapped in crummy red tissue paper with sticker stars all over it.

"What have you got for Caroline?" Tyler asks me.

And James turns. "Yeah, what?"

"Something prime," I say, and the word makes me smile. Prime beef, I think, ready for defrosting.

Chapter 6

No more school till after Christmas. All vacations are good, but Christmas vacation is extra prime and the first day is one of the best.

It's Friday, so Caroline isn't here and that definitely adds to the occasion. Dad and James and I get up early and we're down on the ferry landing at eight to meet the other islanders. There has been snow in the night and Dad says the temperature is about twenty-two.

I'm worried about my mouse marker. I thought I saw it as we passed, a black dot against the smooth whiteness of the snowdrift, but it might have been only a resting bug and there was no way to check it out—not with Dad there. If I lose it my plan's finished, unless of course

I find another mouse, because a dead mouse is definitely what Caroline is going to get.

Most of the islanders are already waiting on the landing when we get there. Harry the Needle is easy to pick out, tall and skinny as a church steeple, his red tasseled cap bobbing on his head. James once said, "Harry looks like a stick of beef jerky, brown and wrinkled." That made me laugh because it was so true.

I see the Gephart family, their twins like Tweedledum and Tweedledee in blue hooded snowsuits. The Flahertys are here, and the O'Jibways except for Fletcher O'Jibway, Debbie's dad. Tyler gives me a mittened high five.

"Where's Fletcher with the sled?" Mrs. Boniface yells.

"He's coming," Mrs. O'Jibway says. "He has to get it ready, you know." She sounds offended.

Now in the distance we hear the tinkle of bells and soon we see Dolly and Daisy, the O'Jibways' two workhorses. Their heavy legs ply the snow; the big sled glides behind them. Mr. O'Jibway is at the helm, as he calls it, and the horses' tails are braided with red ribbons for this special day.

"Whoa Dolly! Whoa Daisy!" he calls, clicking his

tongue and pulling on the reins.

The sled glides to a stop. "All aboard that's coming aboard!" Mr. O'Jibway yells.

Mrs. O'Jibway told us once that when he was a boy, her husband wanted to sail before the mast, but he got seasick on boats and couldn't. Now he's a dry land sailor.

The kids pile on the sled and the men put their big saws and axes and spades and ropes on there too. We're ready.

We skim along Main Street, glad to be riding, laughing at the grownups who trudge behind us, setting their feet in the broad tracks left by the sled.

The Petersons and the Bentsetters and Pastor Lummis have snowmobiles, but they don't bring them. The islanders like doing things the way they've always been done, and we've always done it this way.

Everyone's talking and calling out jokes. Dolly and Daisy toss their heads to make their bells jingle, and their hot breaths drift behind them like smoke.

I love the day we go to get the trees. It's as good as Christmas Day. I tell myself I will not think about Caroline. I will not let her spoil one of the best days of the year.

Tyler, John, and I wrestle about, punching each other, trying to push each other off the sled. We hang over the side and scrape up snow to throw at the girls. They shriek and start scraping too, and pretty soon the snow's flying and we're having a blizzard fight.

At the top of Main Street we turn onto the rutted road that leads up to Dobb's Wood. After a few minutes Mr. O'Jibway calls, "Half speed ahead. Slow. Stop."

Daisy and Dolly know sailor talk, and they stop right away.

"All ashore that's going ashore!" Mr. O'Jibway yells, and Debbie O'Jibway spreads her hands as if to say, "I'm sorry my dad's so goopy," and smiles right at me.

I smile back. It's great to have a joke with Debbie O'Jibway. I'm the one she spread her hands at. I'm the one she smiled at, not Tyler or John Peterson or any of the others.

We jump down.

Mr. O'Jibway has let us off under the trees where the snow is thin on the ground, since most of it has been caught on the branches overhead. We jiggle the trunks so little avalanches drop on us and Debbie O'Jibway sneaks up behind me and crams a handful of snow down the back of my neck.

It's like dry ice, so cold it burns, and I jump and yelp and dance around.

Debbie laughs.

"I'll get you," I growl, but I'm feeling terrific. I think putting snow down a guy's back is probably a good sign.

We need trees for every house on the island, plus forty more to line along Main Street. That's a lot. And we choose carefully, taking from where they grow thickest, making room for new growth.

The air is filled with the buzzing of saws and the sound of falling pines. In a way it's sad to see them come down, but it helps to know we won't only be using them for decoration. After Christmas these same trees will make our ice bridge over to St. Ann's. When the bridge is up, even if it blizzards or fogs or storms, no one need get lost between the island and the mainland. "Stay by the trees and safe you'll be" is a saying that is true even if it doesn't rhyme.

"An ice bridge?" Caroline asked.

"Maybe you'll even help build it," Dad had said to her.

But maybe not.

"Give the Bowsers a big beautiful full tree," Mrs. Boniface orders. "They're having a special Christmas guest this year."

"You mean the Baby Jesus?" one of the Gephart twins asks, all astonished.

"Of course the Baby Jesus, but they're having Mr. Bowser's girlfriend, too," Mrs. Boniface explains.

I hate the way Dad grins and gets all dopey-eyed. He looks like a sick dog. I hope I didn't look like that when Debbie put the snow down my back. I'd die of embarrassment.

"What's a girlfriend?" a twin wants to know.

Everyone thinks that's pretty funny. I keep my face blank and hang on to my secret. With any luck Caroline won't be Dad's girlfriend much longer.

Dolly and Daisy have to make several trips to the island's houses and back.

When we've got all the rest of the trees we need, we stop for hot chocolate and thick slices of Mr. Peterson's Christmas cake. He's a great baker. The cake is filled with nuts and raisins and pieces of bitter orange peel the kids spit out. We try to see who can spit the farthest and every year we search for signs of orange trees growing up in Dobb's Wood, even though we know trees don't work that way.

"I baked an extra cake for you, David," Mr. Peterson tells Dad. "Since it's going to be such a special Christmas. I'll bring it over."

"He's looking to get a wedding cake order," Harry the Needle jokes, and nudges Mrs. Woosam, who's a widow and on the lookout, so Mrs. Boniface says. Mrs. Woosam doesn't laugh. I don't either.

When we've eaten the last of the cake and finished up the hot chocolate, we sleigh-ride back into town to set the trees along Main Street. It's easy to do. We hack holes in the snow where the curb would be and drop the tree trunks in. They freeze in place right away. That tree line is as straight as soldiers on parade. Main Street looks beautiful.

"Just like Fifth Avenue in New York," Mrs. Ludwig says, and Mr. Ludwig says, "Not that we've ever seen Fifth Avenue in New York." Then he blows his nose with his great honk. Tyler and I call him The Honking Goose.

It's almost dark when we drape the last tinsel over the last tree. The island moon hangs high over the bay and when I look up I see stars with other stars behind them, and more behind them. I bet those stars go on forever.

Our trees glitter with frost and tinsel, fine as cobwebs. The shops, their uneven roofs thick with snow, are as make-believe as gingerbread houses. There's not a sound anywhere.

"We sure do live in a pretty place," Harry the Needle says, and someone murmurs, "Amen to that."

We're all suddenly quiet.

"Let's go home, boys," Dad whispers. And he's holding our hands as we call our quiet good-nights.

"Caroline's coming tomorrow," James says happily. "Caroline."

And now I'm thinking about tomorrow because today is over. Tomorrow will be hard. But after that it will be finished.

Chapter 7

Our tree is big and green and beautiful. It stands in the corner farthest from the heat of the stove, waiting for Christmas Eve when we decorate it before we go to church.

Dad and James are getting ready to meet Caroline coming off the ferry, as if she doesn't know the way by now. As if she's helpless or something.

It's so cold James has to have two pairs of socks under his boots, and two sweaters under his jacket. He has Beauty, the cardboard dog, in his pocket.

"Are you coming, George?" Dad asks.

"No," I say, "because I have Christmas gifts to wrap."

This time of year that's always a perfect excuse, and everyone understands secrets.

I watch from the window till they're gone. They take on all kinds of strange shapes through the frost on the glass. It's like looking in the mirrors in the summer fair fun house in St. Ann's.

As soon as they're out of sight I hurry to put on my boots and jacket and cap, and grab one of the spades from the toolshed in case I have to dig.

No kidding, I'm just getting to this mouse in time. One more snowfall and he'd have disappeared till the spring thaw. Either that, or I'd have needed to shovel a ton of snow to find him. The top of the marker is just a faint dot, black on white.

I scrape at the snow with the corner of the spade, careful not to move the twig.

In a couple of minutes I find the mouse corpse. He's worse-looking than ever—dark and wizened—well preserved, though. He's still got a mouse look to him. He'd be admired in any museum.

I take off my cap and wrap him carefully in it, then lay him on the path while I shovel back the snow. I think my ears have fallen off my head, and my nose hurts underneath. I hope it doesn't scab up.

Oh-oh. There's the ferry whistle. I need to hurry. I grab my cap and run down the path, dragging the spade, slipping and sliding because this shortcut isn't used all that much and under the snow the ice is thick.

I'm beginning to think the mouse might be too cozy and warm, so I take him out of my cap and carry him by his tail. His fur is dripping. I'd like to give him a name, but no name I can think of seems right not Mickey, certainly, and not Fluffy or Snowball.

I'm almost home when I see Mrs. Peterson. Her dark-green down coat is ridged like the Michelin Man's, and she's wearing a ski mask. But that's her voice all right.

"George Bowser," she yells. "Are you mad, coming out on a morning like this with your head uncovered?" She's carrying a big tin box with a red poinsettia on it.

Quickly I slide the mouse into my pocket.

"I'm just out for a minute, Mrs. Peterson, to get something." I nod toward the spade. My cap dangles from my hand.

"Put your cap on right now," she says.

I look down at it. It's wet.

"Well." She thrusts the tin toward me. "Here's the fruitcake Mr. Peterson promised. I said I'd take it. You can save me the rest of the walk by bringing it with you."

I take the tin. "Gee, thanks."

"Hurry home," she orders. "We don't want any frost-bitten ears for Christmas."

"No, ma'am." I hurry, all right. "Thanks again," I call back.

Safely home in the kitchen I put the tin on the table, sample a piece of the cake, and save the bits of orange peel to spit later. Then I fish in my pocket for the mouse. My fingers glom onto soaked fur, slick and slimy. "Yucko," I mutter as I wriggle him out. He's yucko, all right. Poor thing. I hold him at eye level, twirling gently, and wonder if he had a heart attack or died of old age. He is pretty dead-looking.

I run up the stairs. The small red Christmas box is ready and waiting with the crisp tissue paper folded back. Last year Dad gave me my first wallet in this red box.

The mouse is awfully wet. I set him on my bed, get a hunk of toilet paper, and blot him off.

Then I lay him in the box, fold the tissue paper over him, snap the gold elastic band in place, and slide the box under my bed.

Not a second too soon, either. Here they come, Dad, James, and Caroline, laughing and talking as they stomp snow from their boots before they come in the kitchen.

"George," Dad calls, and I start downstairs.

Caroline is standing in front of the tree, staring up at it. "Oh my," she says. "It smells of the woods at Christmastime. I've never seen a tree so beautiful."

James runs to take her hand. "We've got the primest perfectest one of all for you. Just for you, Caroline."

She bends down and kisses him. "Thank you, James."

I think maybe she's crying.

Then she sees me on the stairs. "Hello, George."

"Hello." I point to the tin with the red poinsettia on it. "Mrs. Peterson brought the fruitcake. It's good. I've tried a piece."

"Oh, boy." James runs across to open it.

Caroline slices it and we all have some. I have seconds. It sure is good. This piece has four more chunks of peel to add to the others.

"I expect all the nice island ladies look after you

three handsome men," Caroline says.

Quick as anything, I correct her. "Nah, they know we can look after ourselves. We don't need anybody's help. Besides, it was *Mr.* Peterson who baked this."

Dad smiles at me. "Well, sometimes we don't look after ourselves all that well." He puts Caroline's big canvas bag on the couch.

"Presents," he whispers to me, in a fake secret way. "We're to hide them in the cupboard and not look."

"We're to promise not to look." James nods solemnly.

"We've decided not to arrange them around the tree until it's decorated on Christmas Eve," Caroline explains.

There's that "we" again.

"Should I . . . put the whole bag in the cupboard?" Dad asks, but Caroline says, "No. We'll just put the presents in. I need some of the stuff in the bag."

She dips in and reaches three wrapped boxes to James to put in the cupboard.

"Is this one mine?" James is carrying a package big as a shoebox wrapped in blue paper with white snowmen on it.

"No rattling, now. No sniffing," Caroline warns him.

"It is mine. Look." James spells out his name from the card, running his pudgy fingers along the letters.

"And here's Georgie's."

Mine is even bigger, wrapped in silver paper, shiny as airplane wings.

"And this one's yours, Dad." James's eyes sparkle with excitement. Dad's package is long as a pencil box, and James gives it a sneaky little shake. "It's heavy," he says. "Nothing rattles."

Caroline grins her wide grin. "Better put them inside the cupboard and close the door on temptation, James."

I think about my little red box upstairs, and I'm expecting to feel triumphant, but instead there's a twitch of something—maybe fear. Everything's so friendly. They're so friendly. Dad's going to explode when he learns about the mouse. And Caroline, well, I don't know what it is I feel when I imagine Caroline opening the box. I have fear and a sort of warm shame that's mixed with triumph. A little shame or fear is not going to stop me though. My plan is in action. I'm just waiting for my chance. It's now or never. No waiting till Christmas Eve for this little gift, because I have a gut sureness that tells me Caroline is going to be settled in after

Christmas. She'll be our mom.

Everything depends, though, on my getting her alone and that's not going to be easy.

She and James and Dad start making sugar-cookie people, using frosting to give them red Christmas vests.

I say I don't have time to help. I'm painting a stand for Tyler to display his rock collection. It's my Christmas gift to him. This is true, but I could have gone downstairs and made cookie people with them. We all know it.

The smell of sweetness drifts upstairs and Caroline sends James with a hot little sugar guy, red-vested and wrapped in a napkin. I eat his feet first and move upward. He's delicious.

I'm still trying to think of a plan to get Caroline alone, when fate plays into my hands. It's almost as if it's meant to be, and that makes me feel better.

Caroline has a project. She says the old chest of drawers we brought downstairs is really a beauty under all that peeling paint and varnish, and she has started stripping it.

"Extra drawers are always useful," she said when she first saw it. And James asked, "Why? What for?"

Caroline smiled. "Well, for instance, if I'm here for longer than a day or two and bring some more things, I might need more space."

I know James missed the fond look that passed between Caroline and Dad, but I didn't.

She's coming for more than a day or two. After Christmas she's going to stay.

"If they get married and have a baby, they would need more space and more drawers." I can almost hear Tyler saying the words and they burn into my head.

Caroline is working on the chest of drawers this afternoon.

Dad comes upstairs and says he and James are walking down to the bike shop because Caroline needs a paint scraper and he has one down there. "Would you like to come?" he asks me.

I stand my paintbrush carefully in the jar. "Is Caroline going too?" I ask.

I don't look up into the silence, just down at the bright blue line I've painted around the edge of the shelf on Tyler's stand.

"If she's going with us, you're not? Is that it?" Dad asks quietly.

"Au contraire," I say, which is French for "You've got it all wrong." Our fourth-grade teacher used to say that. "I want to finish this." I flash Dad a happy, lying smile.

"Well, she's staying, so you're free to change your mind," Dad says.

"I'm still staying home," I say. My heart is popping and it hurts. Why? This is what I've been waiting for. Dad and James are going, Caroline's staying, she and I are alone, my time has come.

Dad pauses as if he wants to say something more, but he only adds, "It's almost Christmas, Georgie."

Such a strange thing to say, as if I don't know.

"We'll be back in a half hour." He closes the door quietly.

I sit looking at the blue line I've just painted, at the water in the jar that has turned a deep, dark color. My hand is shaking as I take the brush out, wipe its tip on a rag, and leave it on my desk.

I reach under my bed and pull out my present for Caroline.

Chapter 8

Caroline is down on her knees in front of the old chest of drawers. The kitchen is filled with the forest smell of the tree mixed with the tang of the paint thinner. She glances up as I come in and she sees the box.

I accidentally move it a little and the mouse slides around, so I tip it again to get him nicely in the middle.

"Hey," Caroline says, "something else for the cupboard?"

I'm seeing and hearing very clearly. Maybe it's like before an earthquake when even worms can hear the world tremble. For the first time I understand that Caroline and I don't talk to each other easily. We circle and watch. It's been like that since the first day way back. That summer morning when she came to the island, smiling her pumpkin smile, when she and Dad first met.

She's still kneeling, but when I say, "It's for you. It's to open now," she stands up.

"Georgie! Really?" Her face has gone all soft and blurry. I think maybe me giving her a present is making her happy. She probably thinks we'll stop circling now.

She takes the box and bends her head over it. The paint thinner has made her fingers brown.

"Something especially from you to me? That's so nice, George." She wipes her hands on a towel rag and says, "I know. Wait a sec."

I watch her go to the corner cupboard. There's a red ribbon braided in her hair, for Christmas I guess, like Dolly's and Daisy's. Caroline takes out a package and holds it toward me. "And this is especially from me to you."

I don't want to take it, but she thrusts it into my hand. "Here. There's another bigger something for you, for under the tree."

My hands close on the package and I know what it is. I know. My heart starts to tick in a fast, scary way, loud as the tick of the mantel clock.

Caroline sits down on the couch by the stove and pats the place beside her, but I stay put.

"Who goes first?" she asks. "You or me?"

"You." It's so warm in the kitchen that I've started to sweat.

I watch as she slides off the cord and sets the mouse box in her lap.

"I love presents," she says, and lifts the lid.

I can't let her. I can't. I leap forward. "Wait! There's something I forgot."

Too late. She has folded back the paper.

From where I stand, one hand clutching the package she gave me, the other reaching out to stop her, I see the mouse. Wet spreads around him. I should have dried him better before I put him in. Or maybe he's started to thaw. All I can see of Caroline is the top of her head and her bent shoulders.

She doesn't move or scream or anything.

I want to bawl. I want to run away forever. I can't move. At last she looks up.

"You hate me this much, Georgie?"

I stand, turning her package round and round in my

hands, not answering. The smell of the paint thinner is making me sick.

"I don't want to take your mother's place, you know," Caroline says. "I couldn't. She was the love of your father's life and . . . "

If she hadn't mentioned Mom maybe it would have turned out different. "Go away," I whisper. "Don't come back."

And then I run. I run to my bedroom, bang the door, and stand with my face pressed hard against the cold wall.

Below I hear our front door open and I think, Dad's home. He's going to see the mouse. She'll tell. He'll be so mad, sad too. He'll say, "George did what?"

There's no sound of voices. I'm still holding the package she gave me and I toss it on the bed and feel around the wall to the window.

Caroline is walking across the yard. She's wearing her boots and her red-and-gray-plaid parka and she's carrying the box. I watch her take the garden trowel from the wooden table. She'd brought the trowel in the fall, along with a bag of bulbs on one of the gold-leafed days.

"We'll have daffodils for spring," she'd said.

I watch as she goes to where the compost heap lies under its hump of snow.

She trowels out a hole, puts the box in, covers it over.

Burial for a mouse. And there's not even a marker.

At dinner Caroline seems to be the same as ever.

I can't eat.

"Are you sick, Georgie?" Dad asks. "Come over here and let me feel your forehead."

I stand next to him, not looking at Caroline.

"I don't think you're hot," he says. "Caro, what do you think?"

My feet won't move, but Dad gives me a little shove.

Caroline puts her hand against my cheek. I feel her fingers tremble. "No fever," she says, "but maybe he should just go to bed."

I nod.

"I'll come up a little later and see how you're doing," Dad says.

"'Night, Georgie," James calls. "Can I have your pudding if you're not going to eat it?"

I nod again. "Sure."

Caroline doesn't say anything.

I go slowly upstairs. My feet are heavy, almost too heavy to lift. I flop down on the bed.

Caroline's package is still there where I'd tossed it. I stare at it for a long time, and then I get up and slide it unopened under my mattress.

Chapter 9

Tomorrow is Christmas Eve. Caroline will be here for three whole days. Since she didn't tell about the mouse, and since it didn't seem to change her, I expect she'll come. Maybe I've just made everything worse.

On the Advent calendar there's only one shuttered window and the golden door left to open.

I woke up a bunch of times in the night, going over what had happened. I couldn't feel the package under my mattress, but I kept imagining it there and moving myself to the other side of the bed close to the wall. I am like the Princess and the Pea in the story Dad read us once. The pea is under there and I can't forget it.

Tonight after supper Dad goes out as usual to call Caroline.

When he comes back we know something's wrong. He looks as if someone has stomped on him. "Caroline won't be coming for Christmas after all," he says.

My heart jumps. What? Did she tell him? Did she say, "That rotten kid, George"?

James starts to wail and his face bends out of shape. "Why? I want her to come. I want . . . "

I put down my glider and my tube of glue and grip my hands tightly together under the table. "What did she say, Dad?"

Dad's nose is red and when he blows it he sounds loud as Mr. Ludwig, The Honking Goose. "I didn't get to talk to her," he says. "She left a message with her landlady. Her father's ill. She flew to Chicago to be with her mother. She said to tell us she's sorry and to wish us Merry Christmas."

"It won't be merry one bit without Caroline," James sobs, "and we have her presents."

My fingers feel as if they've been caught in a door. I make myself stop squeezing them. Already I'm wondering if her dad is really sick, or if she has gone be-cause of me.

Dad hugs James. "We'll keep her presents safe for her till she comes back," he says.

James mumbles against Dad's chest. "Maybe she won't come back. She likes Chicago. Maybe that guy, the one she was married to, maybe she'll start liking him again and . . . "

"Shhhh," Dad murmurs. His face is all twisted up too.

The insides of the glue tube are oozing out onto the spread newspaper. I screw the cap on quickly. James loves Caroline. They both love her. Well, I don't, and I'm glad she's not coming.

It doesn't seem like the night before Christmas Eve. Dad starts us on a game of Neighbors, but James gets in a muddle and has a tantrum and throws his cards on the floor. James hardly ever has a tantrum.

That night I take the package from under my mat-tress and put it in the bottom drawer of my dresser. I won't look at it. I can't.

Next morning Dad goes out again to call from the True Value store. When he comes back he says he couldn't get through. He says everybody's calling everybody because it's Christmas Eve. He says there's a delay of two hours on phone calls to Chicago.

All day long he keeps trying.

It's snowing hard, little frozen flakes that are almost ice. Wind pelts them against the windows and walls.

Dad tells us the ferry didn't run this morning. The ice pack's too heavy and the wind is blowing too hard.

"Marooned," James says miserably. Usually he shouts it, happy as a bear. Today he isn't happy.

I think, See, it wasn't my fault she didn't come. Not my fault at all.

"I'd have tried Conway Cooper to see if he could fly her over," Dad says, and James and I stare at each other. It shows how much Dad wanted Caroline to be here. The plane ride is for special special times. It costs so much I've never heard of anybody using it unless it's an emergency, like the time Grandma Peterson slipped on the ice and broke her hip.

"Fly Caroline over?" James gasps. "You'd have done that? Wow!"

Dad goes to try the phone again.

We eat the pot roast that's left from yesterday,

but nobody wants much.

James is worrying now that Santa won't make it through the snowstorm either. But Dad tells him Santa's sleigh is made for rough weather. "Don't forget he lives at the North Pole, James," he says.

It's a for-real blizzard now. Fierce and wild as it can get on the island.

After supper we struggled through it to the midnight Christmas Eve service. The trowel Caroline used to bury the mouse is just a white lump on top of the white lump of the table. I'm glad I don't have to see it.

We walk in our single file along Main Street, Dad's big back and shoulders saving us from the worst of the storm. We can hardly see the trees we put up.

Inside the church the heaters are on and the candles make warm shadows on the wooden walls. All the islanders are here. We sing "Silent Night, Holy Night," though the blizzard's screeching around outside and it's anything but silent.

Harry the Needle recites "'Twas the Night Before Christmas," and the Gephart twins sing "When Love Was Born." One of them wets his pants from excitement, but nobody cares.

Debbie O'Jibway gives me a card and says, "Merry Christmas, George." Any other time I'd have been so excited at getting a card from Debbie I might have wet my own pants, but tonight there are too many other things to think about. Probably I'll get excited later.

When it's almost midnight Pastor Lummis tells us it's time to light the candles we've brought from home. We carry them carefully to the altar where the big Christmas wreath hangs. Tonight it's too wild to take them out to the churchyard, and the graves that have been cleared of snow have already been lost again. There is no way to tell one from the other. James and Dad and I each have a candle and we go up and put them in the holders. "For Mom," James and I say. And Dad says, "For Julia."

The choir sings real softly and when they stop we have a little sad silence.

Mr. Peterson has made a big pot of potato-and-fish chowder and he ladles out a bowl for each of us before we leave to walk home.

We wish each other Merry Christmas and people tell Dad, "Too bad Caroline didn't make it." They pat him on the back.

"If she had been here she would have liked it, I bet," James says.

Dad squeezes James's shoulder. "I bet she would have, James. Maybe next year."

But I have this feeling maybe not next year. Maybe not ever.

Chapter 10

Christmas morning. Santa has come. James gets a set of puzzles and a box of Mrs. Santa's fudge that looks and tastes a lot like Annie's.

I get a bunch of stuff, too.

James opens the golden door of the calendar and lifts out Baby Jesus in his manger. The nativity scene is complete.

We stand around it and James says mournfully, "Caroline isn't even here to see."

It's strange, though, how much of Caroline is here, even when she isn't. There's everything to remind us.

The nativity scene, the sugar-cookie people dangling on the tree, James's scarf dangling on the coat rack, the pile of old *Ranger Rick* magazines she'd found in the used bookstore and brought to us. The kitchen is filled with her. There's the chest of drawers she was refinishing. Dad has pushed it against the wall and from somewhere he has found an old red tablecloth to drape over it. We can still smell the paint stripper.

I offer to help carry it back upstairs, but Dad says, "No, we'll just leave it." I know why, even though he doesn't say. Leaving it means she's coming back.

Even though it's Christmas Day, he goes down to phone. But the True Value market is closed, of course. Simon Granville likes to spend at least one day of the year with his wife and his son, Patrick.

We stack the presents under the tree to open after dinner, the way we always do. Then we help Dad fix the turkey and Mom's cranberry salad, and I scrub the skins of the sweet potatoes.

When we set the table I start to go for the dried flowers that are usually in the center, but are now in the empty bedroom. I stop. No use bringing that up.

And then, just when we're about to sit down to eat,

Patrick Granville comes struggling up the path to our door. He's wearing a ski mask and a scarf that's wrapped around that again. "Mrs. Boniface came by to tell us that the phone in the market has been ringing all morning," he yells. Even yelling his voice has trouble making it through all the layers.

"Dad sent me down in case something was wrong. It's for you, Mr. Bowser."

"Come in, Patrick!" Dad shouts.

"No, I'm in a hurry."

"Is it Caroline?" Dad yells.

And Patrick shouts, "It's Chicago, anyway. A terrible connection. But you'd better get a move on. It's costing her bucks."

Dad rushes out without even taking his jacket, and James and I rush after him, thrusting it and his cap and gloves into his hands. "Hurry, hurry," James yells. His face is shining.

When we're back inside, he hops on one foot to the stove and back. "If I do this ten times without putting my foot down, it means she's coming after all," he says.

"That's dumb," I tell him, and I throw myself on the couch, filled with guilt and dread and some crazy kind of hope.

"I bet she's coming on Conway Cooper's plane," James says. "Maybe she'll be here for dinner."

"That's dumb," I say again. "You're such a bozo, James."

He is. He's putting an extra napkin and an extra place setting of silverware on the table.

The windows are so frosted up we can't see through them, so we keep opening the door to check if Dad's coming. Blasts of freezing air filled with pellets of ice blow in and it takes both of us pushing to get the door closed again.

Unexpectedly, then, Dad's back.

"She's calling from the hospital," he says. "Her dad's getting better, but she still feels she has to stay with her mother."

James gasps. "Forever?"

"I don't know, James." Dad pauses. "She says she doesn't know if she could make it work back here with us."

I'm standing by the table spinning one of the spoons on it, not looking at Dad.

"Make what work?" James asks.

"Oh, the loneliness and everything. Being cut off. It's not that she doesn't . . . care about us." Dad pauses again. "Well . . . " His smile is so unreal it makes me want to bawl. "It's Christmas," he says. "Let's be happy."

"I don't want to be happy," James yells. "I want Caroline."

"Don't be such a baby," I tell him. But I rub his back. He loves having his back rubbed.

The turkey is dry as sand and the sweet potatoes have dripped out of their skins and are black crusty balloons on the bottom of the oven. Only Mom's cranberry salad tastes good.

We open our gifts.

Caroline has bought James a boat that looks like the Island Rover and a whistle that blasts the way the Rover's horn blasts. She has given me an ornithopter kit. There's a book telling its history and how the original is in a museum in France. Caroline has written a card: "Leonardo da Vinci was interested in flight too. He held on to his dreams. Hold on to yours, Georgie."

The worst indigestion I've ever had in my life stabs at my chest. I should have known that turkey would do me in.

Dad holds the long narrow little box with his name on it for a minute, then slips it in his pocket. "I'll open it later," he says. "I think she bought me a watch."

We're all miserable, even me.

For the first time we skip the carol singing before bed, because James says he has a bellyache. I think the turkey got him, too.

Later I lie under the bed covers thinking. Well, I got what I wanted. Christmas is over and Caroline didn't come. She's probably gone forever. I wish I felt happier.

I hear Dad pacing up and down in his bedroom next door. Maybe he's like James. Maybe he thinks if he paces wall to wall a jillion times Caroline will come back.

I start counting, but at fifty-four I fall asleep.

Chapter 11

The blizzard blows itself out two days after Christmas, but the ferry has stopped. The in-between days are definitely here.

There's no school for us kids, even after the Christmas holidays are over, and classes have started again on the mainland. Every morning we go to Mrs. Peterson's house for lessons. She used to be a teacher, but it's not like ordinary school. We imagine the St. Ann's kids grumbling and saying, "Those lucky dudes over there on the island." That usually makes us feel terrific, though somehow I don't feel terrific about much these days.

There's lots to do on the island in the in-between

days. We go ice skating and ice fishing up at Mc-
Comber's Pond. There's hill sledding down the Armory
Road from the fort. There's snowshoeing across the
island, and snowmobile races on the frozen meadow
that was once an old hotel's front lawn. Even though
only three families have snowmobiles, it's a dog-eat-dog
competition. For the old people who are brave enough
to venture out, there's bingo in the church hall twice a
week, and there's Saturday night dancing.

Mr. O'Jibway says the in-between days are like being
on a ship at sea. You have to keep busy or go crazy. On
the island going crazy is called "getting rock fever," and
it usually takes a while before it starts. Dad says once it
starts, it grows into an epidemic.

He's painting the two big dining rooms in the Bay
View Hotel and James and I go with him, sometimes
helping, mostly just chasing each other up and down
the staircases and through the empty rooms. It's dark
and spooky because the windows are blocked with snow,
so it's fun to hide and pounce out of closets.

We spend a lot of time at home. I've started making
my ornithopter. It's cool. This guy da Vinci thought he
could strap the ornithopter on his back and fly like a

bird. There are hand bars and leg bars to make the wings flap up and down. He was a dreamer, all right.

I'm doing something else and I don't know why. I'm making a calendar with the moons and the tides and everything, and making it nicer than the one I gave Mrs. Yokum in school. I don't know why I'm being so careful with it, either.

James is keeping a diary to show Caroline. He calls it a dairy. He prints,

>Today it snowed.
>Today it didn't snow.
>Today it snowed again.

I know what's in it, because I have to spell just about every word. It's about the most boring "dairy" ever.

"I'm going to give it to Caroline when she comes back," he says over and over. "Then she won't miss anything. Isn't it prime perfect?"

I glance secretly at Dad.

He looks grim.

One day he says, "I don't think she's coming back, James. She's looking for an apartment in Chicago."

Dad knows this because he calls Caroline all the time. At first I was nervous when he came back from calling her. I would think, maybe tonight she told him about the mouse. But after a while I began to feel secure. It makes me wonder, though, Why doesn't she tell him? In a way I wish she would, because not telling makes her seem nice, and I don't want to think of her as nice.

In spite of keeping busy we can feel rock fever setting in. We're out of heating oil. The shelves in the True Value are as bare as Mother Hubbard's cupboard. We're stingy with our powdered milk and our sugar, and the only kind of fruit we have is the dried kind.

Early every morning Harry the Needle goes down to the bay to check its thickness. Each day he can walk out a little further before a poke of his needle pole causes him to come back shaking his head.

"How's it going, Harry?"

"Any chance of making the ice bridge?"

"Not yet," Harry says. "We need a few more nights as cold as Tuesday's."

We keep at him. "You test the ice today, Harry?"

"I test her every day, goldarn it!"

This time of year Harry the Needle's the most important man on the island and he gets real uppity.

"She's got to have the temperature under fifteen degrees," he tells us impatiently. "For night after night after night. You know that by now. Do you want me to

go through the ice and be lost in the hundred feet of water like the last tester?" Harry snorts.

"No, Harry, we wouldn't want that."

"Then give my head peace."

We pamper him with hot mulled cider and bubble gum, which is his favorite treat.

Some mornings James and I go down to the bay and test the edges of the ice ourselves. We stand on the frozen, slippery dock and stare across at St. Ann's. If you didn't know better, you'd think the bay was a nice, soft, white field covered with ridges and hollows. We do know better. There's ice under there and the dark swirl of water and what's left of the schooner *Miss Julia* that sank in 1832 in the cold windswept waters of the bay.

This morning big dry snowflakes are falling, blurring the church spires and the houses of the island.

The ice looks thick. James takes a step off the dock, snow coming up above his boot. I grab his arm and drag him back.

"Are you crazy? Don't be in such a hurry. It's not ready till Harry the Needle says it's ready."

James is wearing Caroline's scarf. The ends have come loose and I tuck them back and pull his cap over his ears.

"But I am in a hurry," James begins. Then he points. "Look, it's Harry the Needle."

I look, and there he is, halfway across the bay. "Harry!" we shout. "Harry!"

I use my teeth to gnaw off one of my gloves and wave.

Harry lifts his needle high and comes carefully across the frozen bay toward us, stopping every step to test the ice in front of him.

It takes a while for him to get to us. He leans his needle against his chest and wipes his face with the long wet tassel of his red cap. Then he sighs an important sigh.

"Are we ready?" James asks breathlessly.

"She's four inches thick all the way across. Six inches in some places," Harry says. He scrapes ice from his boots with the point of his needle. "We can start getting the trees ready today. And tomorrow if the cold keeps up and the sun don't shine, we can make our bridge."

"Yippee!" James bunnyhops and the dock beneath us creaks, splintering the ice in little sharp pops.

"Quit it, James," I warn.

"We'll see Caroline!" he shouts.

"How do you figure that?" I ask sourly. "You think we're going to make this bridge all the way to Chicago?"

"It's just, we'll be closer to her, that's all." James looks up at me anxiously.

He's so little. I don't know why I have to be so mean to him, anyway. "You're right," I say, giving his back a friendly rub. "We'll be much closer."

Harry the Needle grins. "Over a mile closer, kid, and that's a hard mile. It counts for a heck of a lot of distance." He fumbles off his glove and unwraps a big ball of gum. "I'd share this, but it's already been chewed. Do you guys want to help me ring the church bells?"

"Yeah." James is happy again.

He and I swing on the bell ropes and high above us the big church bell clangs out its message:

Everybody come help get the trees.

Tomorrow we make the bridge.

Ding, dong, ding dong. The in-between days are over.

And tonight, tonight I will do what I couldn't make myself do before. Tonight I will open Caroline's package.

Chapter 12

Everyone comes to help with the trees, even the little Gephart twins.

"Where's Dad?" James asks, peering back toward our house.

"Can you beat it?" Mr. Flaherty asks. "He's stopped to call Chicago again. That man must have shares in the phone company."

He's telling Caroline we're not marooned anymore, I think. He's asking her if she's sure she wants to stay in Chicago. And what is Caroline saying?

"Here's the sled." James grins and wipes his drippy nose on the back of his glove.

"Stop that," I say automatically.

"Hallelujah, we're ready to get started," Mrs. Gephart says. She had her twins three years ago during the in-between days when we were so stuck even the plane couldn't get across. Since then she says it's the relief of her life when the island's open again.

Mr. O'Jibway pulls on the reins, and Dolly and Daisy and the sled come to a stop. The jangling of the horses' bells slows to a tinkle, then fades away.

"All right, you swabbies," Mr. O'Jibway calls. "Hit the deck."

Debbie O'Jibway and Marguerite Boniface are riding with him and they hop down.

I'd forgotten to thank Debbie for the Christmas card the next time I saw her. And then too many days passed and I was too embarrassed. What a weird thing. She seems to like me more now. Tyler and I have pondered this a couple of times and Tyler says maybe it's because now she thinks I'm hard to get and girls are supposed to like that.

"But I'm easy to get," I say, and Tyler shrugs. "We know that, but she doesn't."

Now she says, "Hi, Georgie. How's it going?" as she

jumps off the sled.

"Okay, I guess," I say. Tyler's theory is probably true. I'm not falling over myself to talk to her the way I used to. That was before Caroline and before the mouse, before all my worries.

We start at the top of Main Street and chip and saw the trees from their ice bases. I can't help but notice Debbie O'Jibway always works on the same tree I do.

"Seems no time since we got these from Dobb's Wood," Mrs. Boniface remarks. "How time flies." It's something she says every year, though to tell the truth time drags for most of the islanders after rock fever sets in.

Dad comes when we've towed five of the trees onto the sled.

"Did you talk to Caroline?" James asks.

"Yep," Dad says. "I told her we're starting on the bridge tomorrow. We'll be in St. Ann's by nightfall."

"And . . . ?" I ask. My legs have started to tremble.

"And she says to be careful on the ice."

"Do you think she'll come? Do you think she'll be there when we get there?" James asks. "If she is, it will be so prime perfect."

Dad looks at James and then at me. "Come here, boys."

We moved closer. Around us there's talking and shouting and the rustle of chopped trees sliding across the ice, but between the three of us there's the waiting quiet.

"James, George, I told Caroline that if she doesn't come I won't be calling her anymore."

"Because it costs so much?" James asks. "Mr. Boniface was telling Mr. Flaherty you could have bought a Lear Jet with the money you give the phone company."

Dad smiles a little. "It's not that much. It's just . . . If Caroline will never come, what's the use?"

"Will you stop hoping?" I ask, and something passes between Dad and me. I think he understands that in the beginning I didn't want Caroline here. And what about now? Well, now it's just the same.

"I don't believe I'll ever give up hoping," Dad says.

And James echoes, "I'll never give up hoping." He's copying Dad, but he sounds so adult. I watch him wipe his nose again with his glove, but I don't say anything. I just put both arms around him.

"Are you two guys dancing or what?" Mr. Bentsetter

pokes me in the back. "Let's get to it."

"We're coming," Dad says.

I stand for a minute more, my thoughts clear and formed and cold as snowflakes. I did this. I stopped her. Me.

"Georgie, are you on strike? We need that young muscle," Mr. Flaherty calls. "Let's get cracking."

I get cracking.

It doesn't take long to have Main Street cleared of trees. We'd gotten used to our avenue of snow-covered evergreens. Now the street seems empty and deserted.

We push to help Dolly and Daisy get the sled to the dock where we unload. Tinsel like silver spiders' webs still clings to the tree branches. The tangerines that we'd saved and hung on the trees had been scooped clean by birds and are hulled orange shells, thin as light bulbs. The trees, though, are fresh and green as the day we brought them from Dobb's Wood.

"Tree mountain," James says, gazing at the pile we've made.

"Tree hill, more like," I say. But there are a lot of trees. Now it's time to start going house to house.

"I always think it's nice that we use them twice and

not just for Christmas," Mrs. Boniface says. "The trees will guide us over the ice and keep us safe."

"Safe from drowning." James nods in agreement. "And being eaten up by sharks or being squeezed to death by an octopus."

"Indeed." Mrs. Boniface gives James a look.

He and I have already taken the decorations off our tree so it will be ready when we need it. But as we tip it up to move it out of the corner I find one of Caroline's sugar-cookie people still hanging at the back.

"Can I have it? Can I eat it?" James asks.

"No," I say. "It's too old and it's hard as a rock."

Our tree is too old, too, and the kitchen heat has shriveled it up. Now it's the strange brown-green color of my camouflaged World War II gliders. We slide it out to the sled.

"All hands on deck," Mr. O'Jibway shouts. "Heave ho." And our tree is up with the others.

I race back to close the kitchen door. Dead needles puddle in the empty corner where the tree stood, and brown-green spikes trail across the kitchen floor. The clock isn't ticking. I guess Dad has forgotten to wind it. I get the big brass key from the mantel and do it, ignoring the outside shouts of "What's keeping you, George?" The loud tick sounds good. The kitchen is filled with empty air. If the stove wasn't blazing out its heat, you'd think nobody lived here. It wasn't like that when Caroline was here, I think, and something sad moves inside me.

Quickly I turn away.

There are two tree hills now by the frozen bay. It's dark and a pale ice fog creeps ghostlike between us and the mainland. The lights of St. Ann's come and go through it like winter fireflies.

"I hope that fogs lifts itself by morning," Harry the Needle says. "If it doesn't, the bridge will have to be put off for another day. I'm not taking no people with me on the ice in no fog." He chews hard and blows a bubble, big as a baseball.

We're all silent, except Mrs. Gephart, who gives a moan.

Tyler whispers to me, "I bet she's having more twins."

"Be here by seven in the A.M.," Harry the Needle orders in his in-between days bossy voice.

"We'll be here," we say.

———

That night, before I get into bed I take Caroline's package from the bottom drawer, tear it open, and take out the scarf. It's blue-and-white striped, same as James's, but it's way longer. I think maybe it has more mistakes, too, because Caroline had more chances to mess up with it being longer. I guess she didn't get better with practice. There's a hole halfway down I can stick two fingers through. When I hold it above my head, it trails on the ground. It's as if Caroline started it and didn't want to stop.

I remember when she was knitting the one for James, the way she'd look up and say, "Goshdarn, another mistake and I don't know how to fix it." Then she'd laugh and say, "Oh, well." I remember the way her face got red when she sat close to the stove. The way she'd push her hair back. She must have done this for me at night, after work, sitting in her room in St. Ann's. I poke my fingers through the hole, halfway down, and imagine her saying, "Goshdarn. Another mistake. A person has to love a person a lot to go to all this bother, not to mention do all this knitting." And suddenly I'm crying.

I hold the scarf against my face and cry and cry. And when I get into bed I take the scarf in with me.

Chapter 13

The morning is filled with dark and blowing snow. Dad and James and I walk toward the dock.

I'm wearing Caroline's scarf.

"Where did you get it?" James had asked when I appeared in it after breakfast.

"She left it for me," I told him, and Dad said quietly, "It took you a long time to start wearing it, George."

"It took a long time," I said.

Now as we wade along Main Street I snuggle my chin into the scarf and sniff at the wet wool. It smells so good. I'm all weighted down on one side with the money in my pocket, and I keep my arm tight against my side in case it rattles.

When we pass the True Value store I call out to Dad, "I have to go in the market. See you at the dock."

Dad nods.

"You should have gone before we left home. I did," James says, all pious.

I don't bother to tell him that when I said I needed to go it wasn't the kind of needing to go he was imagining.

The True Value isn't open for business because Simon Granville and Patrick will be down at the dock ready to help with the ice bridge. They know there'll be no customers. But the market isn't locked on tree day, in case someone needs the bathroom or has some other emergency.

I shake myself off and go inside.

The True Value is dank and cold and not like itself. The shelves have that empty, hungry, in-between days look. I drag off my gloves and fumble the pile of change from my pocket. There's a bunch of it, all right. I've raided my baseball bank during the night and I have seven dollars and sixty cents, all in quarters and nickels and dimes.

The phone is on the wall in the corner on a black metal stand with air holes over it. I never figured out why the air holes are on the stand. There's a black metal shelf that holds a pile of phone books.

I spread my change on the shelf, dropping half of it because my fingers are so cold; then I start searching for the Chicago phone book. There isn't one. I stand baffled.

"Information," I say out loud, and I put in some money and when the voice asks for what city, I tell her.

She tells me I have to dial another number. But then I'm talking to the information guy in Chicago.

"We have no Caroline Best," he says.

"Could you look again, please?" I ask. "I know she's there. That's where she lives with her parents."

He interrupts. I can tell he's a very very busy person, because he hardly lets me finish my sentence. "Could it be under another name? Do you know her address?"

"No, but could you just . . . "

"Have you any idea how many Bests there are in this city?" The guy clips his words like he's clipping his nails. "Sorry, I can't help you."

And he's gone.

I stand staring at a poster on the wall that shows sunshine and palm trees and a sandy beach. California raisins in white gloves are dancing their brains out. I want to cry. I can't talk to Caroline. I can't tell her.

The St. Ann's phone book is right on top. St. Ann's is worth a try. If she started to come after Dad called . . .

My icy fingers have trouble with the pages, but I find her name, put in the money, and hear the phone ring. My insides are crawling. What if I hear her voice right now? It's early. What if I'm waking her up?

The phone's ringing and there's a click. I hope I'm not going to throw up. The bathroom's way back behind the counter.

"This is Caroline Best." It's a robot voice, but it still has some of Caroline's smile in it. "I'm sorry I can't take your call right now, but please leave a message after the beep."

My eyes drift over the raisin poster without ever coming in for a landing. There'll be a beep, and then what will I say? All the things I'd planned to tell her have flown away.

Beep.

"Caroline?" I swallow. "Caroline, I'm sorry about the

mouse." I stick my finger in one of the black metal holes that surround the phone. It's not as big as the hole in my scarf. "Thank you for the scarf and the ornithopter. We miss you." I try not to whimper. "Dad's . . . "

There's a click. She's gone.

Now I'm remembering my speech. It was so much better. Should I call again? Does one message cancel out another? I'll practice. I'm standing, mouthing words, when Patrick comes in the market.

"Hi." I can tell he's surprised.

He grins as I move quickly from the phone. "Oh ho, what am I seeing here? Have you got a girl in St. Ann's, Georgie?"

I shake my head. I don't think my voice is working, anyway.

"I thought you liked Debbie O'Jibway." Patrick's going in the back storeroom, talking over his shoulder. When he comes back he's carrying a carton and a small plastic bag.

I'm still standing there.

"Dad sent me for this box of trail mix," he says. "We saved it for the bridge making." He holds up the bag. "Bubble gum. Got to keep Harry the Needle happy."

"Yeah," I say.

"Coming?"

He waits while I gather up my change from the shelf and the floor.

"Want a piece of gum?" he asks, and I say, "Sure," and pick one out. I bite it in half and wrap the other half for James.

"What about the fog?" I ask.

"It's lifted. Harry says we're on our way." Patrick sets down the carton while he pulls on his ski mask.

I wind my scarf up around my ears. It's long enough so it goes to the top of my head like a turban.

"Man," Patrick says, "I can't wait to get over to St. Ann's. The first thing Dad and I are going to bring back is fresh milk. People get real ornery when we're out of fresh milk."

"I bet," I say, though I didn't think we missed it all that much.

Dark figures are gathered around the two tree hills. The three snowmobiles are there too, their headlights reaching out to St. Ann's, their yellow beams not getting far in the white falling blur.

I see Dolly and Daisy and the sled with its big tent

tarpaulin. There'll be blankets under there and thermos bottles of chowder and coffee and plenty of sandwiches. That's where the kids wait, with a couple of mothers to keep order. The younger ones, like James, play cave and spaceship and submarine. The older guys get a card game going and act up to impress the girls. Harry the Needle won't let any kids on his ice till the bridge is up, and we're content to stay on the edge and be safe.

I see Harry now, holding his needle high like a harpoon, the light from one of the snowmobiles shearing off its bright steel.

I give James his half of the gum and he says, "Oh, yum, prime perfect. Thank you, Georgie."

Dad's standing on his own, staring across the ice. He looks so lonely. I wish my ornithopter was real instead of just a model. I'd lend it to him and let him fly to Caroline.

I touch his arm.

He turns and says, "Oh, hi." It's as though he's coming back from someplace else.

"Dad?" I say. "Dad, I want to help make the bridge."

"Help make the bridge?" he repeats, as if he doesn't understand. "You did help, George. Everyone helped bring the trees here, same as always."

I interrupt. "I want to go across the ice, Dad. It's important."

"You know you can't. It's dangerous. Harry the Needle won't . . . "

"It's not that dangerous if I stay next to you, and I promise, promise, promise I will. Harry might say okay if you ask him." I'm chewing so furiously on the gum my cheeks ache.

Dad puts his hands on my shoulders. "Why this terrible need to go, Georgie?"

I try not to look away from his eyes, though it's hard. Snow falls between us, darkens the shoulders of Dad's green parka. His sleeves, his gloves. One snowflake melts on his nose. "Because I gave Caroline a dead mouse for Christmas," I whisper. "I told her to go away and never come back." My heart seems to stop. My breathing. Even the snow seems to stop. "I thought she'd take Mom's place and you'd love her more than you love us."

Dad pulls my face against the front of his soaking wet parka, and his gloved hand rubs my back, the way I rub James's. Not much wonder James likes this. It feels so good, so soothing.

"I love . . . loved Caroline in a different way," he says. "Never more than you. Never more than I loved your mother. Never."

We rock together and that's soothing too. I could almost go to sleep, standing right here, the snow hiding us from everyone else.

Then I sense him stiffen. "Harry," he calls. "I need to talk to you a minute."

I pull away to look.

Harry the Needle's going past us, not stopping. "If there's a problem, sort it out with the rest of them. I have my job to do."

"No problem. My son wants to make the bridge with us, that's all."

Harry doesn't even slow. "Uh-uh. No way."

Dad's following him.

I'm following Dad.

"I'll be responsible for him. He'll be right next to me every step of the way."

Harry peers at me. "George, what's the matter with you? You want to get lost on the ice? Or slip through a crack? Or step out on mush and be gone from here to eternity?"

I shake my head. "I just want to make the bridge."

"This is important, Harry, to both of us," Dad says, very very quietly.

Harry the Needle's an uppity old coot, but he's wise. He strokes the edge of his needle against his face so hard I can hear it rasp on the beard stubble. "It is, eh?" He rasps his face some more. "And you'll be with young George every step of the way?"

Dad smiles at me. "Always was and always will," he says.

"And you, George, you'll hold close to your dad?"

"I promise," I say. We sound the way Debbie's sister and the guy from St. Ann's sounded at their wedding ceremony this past summer, looking at each other, so seriously, making such serious promises. It's serious all right.

"Okay then." Harry the Needle squints across the ice. "You two get a tree and stay behind me. Don't move till I say move. Understood?"

"Understood."

Dad and I watch Harry poke his way onto the ice and then we run back, slipping and sliding to get the first tree.

Chapter 14

Harry's needle stabs the ice. Where he walks, we walk. Where he stops and points we lay down the tree we're dragging.

Mr. Bentsetter is behind us with a pick.

Dad has the trowel. The one Caroline used to bury the mouse. The handle of the trowel was sticking up under the snow on the table and he has found it and brought it with him.

I take it and help Mr. Bentsetter scoop a hole in the ice wide enough for the tree trunk and deep enough so the tree can slide through. Its bottom branches catch and spread on the icy surface and the tree stands straight, already freezing in place.

We're about twenty big paces from the island, not that we took twenty big paces, more like a hundred baby steps.

"The first one's in," Dad yells in the direction of the snowmobile headlights and the islanders who are already only vague shapes behind us.

They cheer, and a voice that's definitely Mrs. Gephart's yells, "Praise be. Keep those trees moving."

Harry the Needle crunches on. He has no time to stop for celebrations. Mr. O'Jibway and Pastor Lummis and Mrs. Boniface reach us for the second planting, pacing carefully where we've paced, touching the first tree for luck as they pass. They touch Dad and me, too, as we head back for a third tree.

The pastor's mustache is hanging with icicles.

We go and come, go and come, walking in the steps of those who've come and gone before us.

Digging the holes is like digging concrete. The work sweats us. The sweat freezes. The snow falls on us. Our eyebrows are white, our noses damp.

We move in a cold cloud of our own fogged breath,

and all the time I'm wondering, Will she be there? If not, will she come? Sometimes Dad and I look at each other without speaking. We're both hoping.

Now and then we stop at the covered sled to dry our faces, drink hot chocolate, and tell the others how far we've gone, though they pretty well know. They're keeping count, and Mrs. Peterson is talking about "multiplication and division of distance." "See how important math can be, Tyler, John, George?" she tells us.

Tyler whispers, "Listen to her. Once a teacher, always a teacher."

The kids on the sled are filling paper cups with snow to make snow cones. Tyler offers me one that is lemon-colored. It's pale yellow.

"Dolly and Daisy made it for you," he says and almost falls down giggling. "You know how horses make yellow snow."

I drop it like a hot potato and Debbie O'Jibway says, "Tyler Flaherty, you're a major gross out."

She gives me a new cup filled with hot mulberry juice and when I look down I see she's drawn a heart on the side of the cup with her initials and mine inside.

"Ah, thanks a lot."

Debbie's wearing her cute white earmuffs and her black jacket with the white reindeer on it. The part of her hair I can see has brush tracks in it as if she's just prettied herself up and she sure has done a good job. She looks really prime, except for the two big cold sores on her lip, and of course she can't help those. Anyway, they're only temporary.

I drink every bit of the juice and give her back the cup. "Keep it for me, okay?" I ask. I can't think when I ever said anything so romantic.

It's late afternoon now and darkening down. Harry says we're three quarters of the way there. The sky is dappled black and gray, hanging low with the weight of the snow it's holding.

We're slowing. If it weren't for the trees to guide us, we'd never find the way back. The island has gone completely. We're in a white world and we watch out for each other. Now and then The Honking Goose that is Mr. Ludwig honks. No one ever moves alone. When I listen I think I hear the cracking of the ice, and sometimes I think I feel the currents of the bay swirling beneath my boots. We're tired. We plod like old, finished horses.

"Okay to go on?" Harry the Needle asks. "Or do we go back and start tomorrow where we left off?"

It's Dad who answers first. "Let's go on."

"Don't give up the ship, boys," Mr. O'Jibway says. He and Mrs. O'Jibway have come with lanterns for us. We've tracked the swing of the lights across the snow. "If I'm not mistaken," he adds, "I just got a glimpse of land off the starboard bow."

We squint where he's pointing. The snow has lazed off a bit and we're close enough to see the murky outline of St. Ann's and people shadows on the dock. Some of the mainlanders come down every year to welcome us, the way people do a long-distance runner at the end of a race. One of them has brought a flashlight.

I'm sick with worry again. Is Caroline one of those ghost shapes? I'm praying that she is. But if she is, what's going to happen to me?

"Let's keep them moving, men," Harry says.

Mr. O'Jibway offers him a lantern, but Harry doesn't want it. "I can smell thick ice," he says.

The lanterns spill their light on the snow, making it yellow as the snow cone Dolly and Daisy made for me. They shine up into the feathery fans of the trees, dance on the shreds of silver tinsel. The bay beyond seems blacker.

I keep looking toward St. Ann's, looking for Caroline's red-and-gray-plaid parka, hoping to see it, hoping not to see it. I don't know anymore.

"Three more trees should do it," Harry the Needle says.

Three.

Suddenly Dad stands straight and shouts, "Caroline, Caroline Best."

The loudness of the shout scares me. It echoes off the ice.

"David . . . " A voice answering, spreading itself in the distance.

I'm breathing funny.

Dad takes a step forward and Harry the Needle catches his arm. "Easy, man, easy. We're not there yet. Your boy doesn't want to lose you on the last lap."

His needle pokes in front of him like a blind man's cane. His hand feels for the depth as he pulls it out of the ice. "Tree here," he says. "Two more to go."

Two.

And Caroline's waiting. Did she get my message?

Did that help persuade her? If she came straight from Chicago she doesn't know I'm sorry. What will she say?

"Another tree and we're there," Harry calls.

One. One more.

Dad has new energy. He's working like a wild man. Every minute he stops and calls, "Caroline," and she calls, "David." It's as if they're afraid of losing each other again. Her voice is getting closer.

Mr. Bentsetter nudges me. "They'll be singing to each other in a minute, the way they do in operas." He nods toward the shore and there's Caroline in a big waterproof poncho and a dripping hat. Her hand is pressed against her mouth.

"Somebody else can set in this last tree," Harry says. "You go, David."

Dad slides over the ice and scrambles up on the dock.

Harry pushes me. "You, too, young George."

I move slowly, stopping to scrape frozen snow from my boots.

Dad and Caroline are hugging.

"I'll never let you be lonely," Dad says, and he's not even whispering.

"I was so lonely in Chicago, right there in the city, I thought I'd die," Caroline says. "I wanted you. You and the boys."

And then she sees me. She holds out her arm, the one that isn't around Dad, and calls, "George?"

When I don't move, she says, "I got your message. Thank you."

"What message?" Dad asks, but he doesn't care. He doesn't care about anything.

"Come," Caroline says.

Something inside me unknots. I make this little sound and I run and she's hugging me, too.

"The in-between days are over," I say, my face sliding against the wet slickness of her poncho. "Will you come back to the island?"

"You made the bridge, Georgie," she whispers. "I'll cross it with you."

I look up and even in the dark I can see her smile.

I sigh. "Prime," I whisper. "Prime perfect."

Eve Bunting is the winner of the 1976 Golden Kite Award and the recipient of the 1977 Best Work of Fiction Award of the Southern California Council on Literature for Children and Young People. Her recent books for HarperCollins include *Is Anybody There?*, a 1989 nominee for the Edgar Award given by the Mystery Writers of America; *Our Sixth-Grade Sugar Babies*, a Best Book of 1990 (*School Library Journal*); *Sharing Susan*; *Coffin on a Case*, winner of the Edgar Award for the Best Juvenile Mystery of 1993; and *Nasty, Stinky Sneakers*.

Ms. Bunting, the author of over one hundred books, was born in Ireland and since 1958 has lived in Southern California, where she works as a lecturer.

Alexander Pertzoff is a free-lance artist whose work has been exhibited in many galleries, in both group and individual shows. He has also illustrated *Three Names* by Patricia MacLachlan. He lives on a farm in western Massachusetts.